Penguin Suit

Kelly Doudna

Illustrated by Neena Chawla

Consulting Editor, Diane Craig, M.A./Reading Specialist

ABDO
Publishing Company

Published by ABDO Publishing Company, 4940 Viking Drive, Edina, Minnesota 55435.

Printed in the United States.

Credits
Edited by: Pam Price
Curriculum Coordinator: Nancy Tuminelly
Cover and Interior Design and Production: Mighty Media
Photo Credits: Peter Arnold, Comstock, Creatas, Digital Vision, Getty Images, ShutterStock

Library of Congress Cataloging-in-Publication Data

Doudna, Kelly, 1963-
    Penguin suit / Kelly Doudna ; illustrated by Neena Chawla.
        p. cm. -- (Fact & fiction. Animal tales)
    Summary: Pancho begins a new job as a waiter at the Emperor Room seafood restaurant, but not without facing some difficulties. Includes facts about penguins.
    ISBN 1-59679-957-9 (hardcover)
    ISBN 1-59679-958-7 (paperback)
    [1. Waiters and waitresses--Fiction. 2. Restaurants--Fiction. 3. Penguins--Fiction.] I. Chawla, Neena, ill.
II. Title. III. Series.

    PZ7.D74425Pen 2006
    [E]--dc22

                                                                                            2005027838

SandCastle Level: Fluent

SandCastle™ books are created by a professional team of educators, reading specialists, and content developers around five essential components—phonemic awareness, phonics, vocabulary, text comprehension, and fluency—to assist young readers as they develop reading skills and strategies and increase their general knowledge. All books are written, reviewed, and leveled for guided reading, early reading intervention, and Accelerated Reader® programs for use in shared, guided, and independent reading and writing activities to support a balanced approach to literacy instruction. The SandCastle™ series has four levels that correspond to early literacy development. The levels help teachers and parents select appropriate books for young readers.

Emerging Readers
(no flags)

Beginning Readers
(1 flag)

Transitional Readers
(2 flags)

Fluent Readers
(3 flags)

These levels are meant only as a guide. All levels are subject to change.

FACT & FiCTiON

This series provides early fluent readers the opportunity to develop reading comprehension strategies and increase fluency. These books are appropriate for guided, shared, and independent reading.

FACT The left-hand pages incorporate realistic photographs to enhance readers' understanding of informational text.

FiCTiON The right-hand pages engage readers with an entertaining, narrative story that is supported by whimsical illustrations.

The Fact and Fiction pages can be read separately to improve comprehension through questioning, predicting, making inferences, and summarizing. They can also be read side-by-side, in spreads, which encourages students to explore and examine different writing styles.

FACT OR FiCTiON? This fun quiz helps reinforce students' understanding of what is real and not real.

SPEED READ The text-only version of each section includes word-count rulers for fluency practice and assessment.

GLOSSARY Higher-level vocabulary and concepts are defined in the glossary.

SandCastle™ would like to hear from you.

Tell us your stories about reading this book. What was your favorite page? Was there something hard that you needed help with? Share the ups and downs of learning to read. To get posted on the ABDO Publishing Company Web site, send us an e-mail at:

sandcastle@abdopublishing.com

Penguins in the wild live only in the southern hemisphere.

Pancho Penguin arrives at the Emperor Room seafood restaurant for his first day of work as a waiter. "You seem like a nice young penguin," the manager, Ms. King, says. "I know you'll do well."

5

When penguins are in the water, their coloring makes it difficult for predators to see them.

The assistant manager, Mr. Humboldt, fits Pancho for a black tuxedo coat, white ruffled shirt, and bow tie. "All the waiters wear these penguin suits," Mr. Humboldt says.

Penguins return to the same site to breed each year. Most rockhopper penguins even use the same nest from year to year.

Pancho's first customer is Mr. Hopper,
a frequent diner at the Emperor Room.
Mr. Hopper sits at his usual table.

"Welcome to the Emperor Room. My
name is Pancho, and I'll be your waiter
today," Pancho says
with a smile.

9

Penguins eat mainly seafood. They hunt for fish, krill, and squid in the water.

"You must be new. All the other waiters know that I always start with shrimp cocktail," Mr. Hopper barks impatiently. "And bring extra cocktail sauce!"

"Yes sir," Pancho replies nervously.

Penguins are graceful swimmers, but they waddle when they walk.

Pancho goes through the in door that swings into the kitchen. He puts a plate of shrimp cocktail and a large bowl of cocktail sauce on his tray. He waddles back toward the in door to go out to the dining room.

IN OUT

13

Penguins that live in warmer climates stay cool by holding out their wings to let body heat escape and to shade their feet.

14

Just as Pancho reaches out to open the door, Ms. King pushes it from the other side. The door smashes into Pancho and knocks him over. His tray flies through the air.

15

Macaroni penguins were named for their crest of yellow forehead feathers, which reminded people of the fancy hats that were popular in the 1700s.

"Pancho! This door is
for entering the kitchen,"
Ms. King scolds. "Use the other one to go out."

Pancho stands up. "I'm so sorry," he says,
crestfallen.

17

Penguins molt each year. They remain on land while their new feathers grow in.

Ms. King says, "Pancho, I can tell you're a good kid. Let's get you into a clean shirt, and I'll give you another chance."

"Thank you. I know I can do better!" Pancho exclaims. "I won't let you down!"

FACT or Fiction?

Read each statement below. Then decide whether it's from the FACT section or the Fiction section!

  1. Penguins in the wild live only in the southern hemisphere.

  2. Penguins work as waiters at restaurants.

  3. Penguins dress in tuxedo coats and ruffled shirts.

  4. When penguins are in the water, their coloring makes it difficult to see them.

Penguins in the wild live only in the southern hemisphere.

When penguins are in the water, their coloring makes it difficult for predators to see them.

Penguins return to the same site to breed each year. Most rockhopper penguins even use the same nest from year to year.

Penguins eat mainly seafood. They hunt for fish, krill, and squid in the water.

Penguins are graceful swimmers, but they waddle when they walk.

Penguins that live in warmer climates stay cool by holding out their wings to let body heat escape and to shade their feet.

Macaroni penguins were named for their crest of yellow forehead feathers, which reminded people of the fancy hats that were popular in the 1700s.

Penguins molt each year. They remain on land while their new feathers grow in.

9
10
18
26
36
44
48
56
62
69
72
81
92
95
103
110
119
128
133

Pancho Penguin arrives at the Emperor Room seafood restaurant for his first day of work as a waiter. "You seem like a nice young penguin," the manager, Ms. King, says. "I know you'll do well."

The assistant manager, Mr. Humboldt, fits Pancho for a black tuxedo coat, white ruffled shirt, and bow tie. "All the waiters wear these penguin suits," Mr. Humboldt says.

Pancho's first customer is Mr. Hopper, a frequent diner at the Emperor Room. Mr. Hopper sits at his usual table.

"Welcome to the Emperor Room. My name is Pancho, and I'll be your waiter today," Pancho says with a smile.

"You must be new. All the other waiters know that I always start with shrimp cocktail," Mr. Hopper barks impatiently. "And bring extra cocktail sauce!"

"Yes sir," Pancho replies nervously.

Pancho goes through the in door that swings into the kitchen. He puts a plate of shrimp cocktail and a large bowl of cocktail sauce on his tray. He waddles back toward the in door to go out to the dining room.

Just as Pancho reaches out to open the door, Ms. King pushes it from the other side. The door smashes into Pancho and knocks him over. His tray flies through the air.

"Pancho! This door is for entering the kitchen," Ms. King scolds. "Use the other one to go out."

Pancho stands up. "I'm so sorry," he says, crestfallen.

Ms. King says, "Pancho, I can tell you're a good kid. Let's get you into a clean shirt, and I'll give you another chance."

"Thank you. I know I can do better!" Pancho exclaims. "I won't let you down!"

GLOSSARY

crestfallen. feeling shamed and low-spirited

molt. to periodically shed feathers, fur, or another outer covering

penguin suit. slang for tuxedo

predator. an animal that hunts others

southern hemisphere. the half of the earth that is south of the equator

tuxedo. a man's dress jacket, usually black, worn with a white shirt and bow tie

waddle. to sway from side to side while taking short steps

To see a complete list of SandCastle™ books and other nonfiction titles from ABDO Publishing Company, visit www.abdopublishing.com or contact us at: 4940 Viking Drive, Edina, Minnesota 55435 • 1-800-800-1312 • fax: 1-952-831-1632